BIGFOOT MYSTERY MAGAZINE   CHRISTMAS

BIGFOOT MYSTERY MAGAZINE CHRISTMAS ISSUE 2022

Ray Harwood's
BIGFOOT MYSTERY MAGAZINE

PAPER BACK

2022 Issue 4

CHRISTMAS SPECIAL EDITION

(The World's first Bigfoot Christmas Magazine issue!)

"Once you have eliminated the impossible, whatever remains, however improbable, must be the truth" –MR. Spock: USS Enterprise.

Contact: figflint@yahoo.com

2022 Copyright

Special thanks to Steve Baxter and Daniel Perez

BIGFOOT MYSTERY MAGAZINE is a review of Bigfoot research and collection crypto related story lines regarding the alleged American relict hominoid known as Bigfoot and as close to factual research data as possible; all attempts were made to properly site, quote and reference. All practical attempts were made to verify the information collected was accurate. Bigfoot is either a mythical creature or an endangered species of American primate or great ape. If you have any sort of encounter contact the BFRO (Bigfoot Field Research Organization), this information is critical to the overall database.

Warning: Wild animals are dangerous, and our working with stone, and can cause injury and death, BMM does not encourage going into the wilderness, if you do so it is on your own accord. In reading this publication you understand to "hold harmless" all whom contribute to this publication.

"Mythology doesn't leave footprints". - Daniel Perez…

WE WILL BE KNOWN FOREVER BY THE TRACKS WE LEAVE" – Santee Sioux Nation

PRINTED IN THE UNITED STATES OF AMERICA

HELP IS AVAILABLE WE CARE! SUICIDE CRISIS LIFELINE DIAL 988

ALSO PLEASE WATCH THE CHOSEN FREE, WE HAVE PAID FORWARD FOR YOUR APP AND STREAMING:
https://watch.angelstudios.com/thechosen
COME AND SEE WHO JESUS WAS AND IS, 'HE HAS CALLED YOU BY NAME": PERFECT PEOPLE- NEED NOT APPLY

FAIR USE: Copyright Disclaimer under Section 107 of the Copyright Act 1976, allowance is made for "fair use" for purposes such as criticism, comment, news reporting, teaching, scholarship, and research. Fair use is a use permitted by copyright statute that might otherwise be infringing. Educational research such as this journal tips the balance in favor of fair use. All art illustrations and art are or research and study purposes.

BIGFOOT MYSTERY MAGAZINE	CHRISTMAS ISSUE 2022

BIGFOOT MYSTERY MAGAZINE — CHRISTMAS ISSUE 2022

BIGFOOT MYSTERY MAGAZINE   CHRISTMAS ISSUE 2022

BIGFOOT MYSTERY MAGAZINE   CHRISTMAS ISSUE 2022

BIGFOOT MYSTERY MAGAZINE   CHRISTMAS ISSUE 2022

Wonder

10 | Page

BIGFOOT MYSTERY MAGAZINE   CHRISTMAS ISSUE 2022

BIGFOOT MYSTERY MAGAZINE   CHRISTMAS ISSUE 2022

Wonder

BIGFOOT MYSTERY MAGAZINE   CHRISTMAS ISSUE 2022

13 | Page

BIGFOOT MYSTERY MAGAZINE   CHRISTMAS ISSUE 2022

"BABY IT'S COLD OUTSIDE!"
2014 in Northern Minnesota

Christmas Bigfoot Encounter

Northern Minnesota Christmas Bigfoot Encounter YouTube

The most famous Bigfoot encounter I could find on Christmas was in 2014 in Northern Minnesota and is still up on YouTube ("North by Wildwest"). 2,586,671 views, posted Oct 3, 2016. There are 6,067 comments on the video thus far. A Sasquatch walks around the house and yard. The dog goes after the Bigfoot but runs back inside. After the animal leaves the property the family goes inside slightly frightened. The film starts inside the house with a Christmas party; the family dog is barking up a storm and darting towards the tree line and back. The Bigfoot, real or not, is on the edge of the property at the tree line. If it was out here in Northern Idaho someone would have shot it, hung it up and butchered it into steaks in the first few seconds, but in the film cell phones were deployed as the choice and several were filming. It felt realistic to me so I send it over to some expert Bigfooters to look at and scrutinize. Most Bigfooters don't respond to me very often, but fortunately I did get several responses from some of the upper tear on this message.

Legendary Bigfooter, Daniel Perez, was kind enough to take the time and look at the film for me. He said "The YouTube video looks very good. Whatever is back there it is hard to make heads or tails of. Is there a real name and phone# associated with the witness?" So it sounds like he is looking into the matter, Daniel is a bloodhound!

Richard Freeman, Zoological Director at Centre for" Fortean" Zoology and former Father Christmas at Great Grottos event Management Company in Dorking England, also was kind enough to inspect the film. Richard wrote back the following:

"The dog's reaction looked real. The figure looks large and takes long strides. But it's too far away and not clear enough to be sure. It seemed to have very long arms from the fleeting glimpses we caught of it too."

Steven Streufort, of Bigfoot Books and "Critical Thinking," was of course highly critical, you have to get through his crew if you wish to cut the mustard of a Bigfoot encounter. He knows his Bigfooting ! Steven was also kind enough to respond:

"Human! Consensus back then was that it was just a Holiday's gag. When you see a crappy video it's useless even if it might be real. That one just looks like a human, so why bother thinking otherwise? "

I came to no firm conclusion as of yet, Steven Streufort stated it looked like a human; humans are in fact the most dangerous animal on earth, so why not call out "who goes there?" A humanoid shape running around is a threating occurrence, that's why people have alarms, fences, dogs and guns! If it were human, or an ape, protecting the family would be priority one, not filming the subject, this being why there is no really good film, except the PG film, when the riffle came out before the camera! On the other hand, many witness reports from similar encounters in that area describe Bigfoot as a human with hair all over. "It walked upright like a man but was covered with fur"(BFRO Minnesota report #67381)

I once worked on a farm in Viking, Minnesota, very far north, they had one old 22 riffle that the owner had made out of old John Deer tractor parts, but they did have one, even though they were democrats (joke lol). No one in the film called out a warning, no one made ready to defend (except the dog). The dog did not seem know the scent of the intruder, however, the dog acted like my dog does when a moose is about the area except the Minnesota dog did not stand his ground, my dog never turns his back on a foe, but has not faced a Bigfoot.

Legendary Bigfooter, Daniel Perez, concurs with Steven Streufort; "Whatever is back there it is hard to make heads or tails of." I also concur with Richard Freeman "it's too far away and not clear enough to be sure. It seemed to have very long arms from the fleeting glimpses we caught of it too." Long arms is a key observation in similar encounters in this state, "the arm length was longer than human's", states northern Minnesota BFRO report #62558 from November 1995 and "arms swinging and hands down to his knees" northern Minnesota BFRO report #59346 April 2018.

So if it were a hoax the subject has studied Bigfoot to some degree. Freeman continues, "The dog's reaction looked real. The figure looks large and takes long strides." Again, the alleged actor did his homework if it is a prank. I had my wilderness danger radar go off, like when I see a range bull, bull moose or bear, if I had to do a SWAG (scientific wild ass guess) based on the human-like subject I would say it is a young bull squatch that smelled the women and holiday food, based on the humans' reaction in I would say it is a prank or Hoax. None of the three expert researchers I asked would hang their squatching hat on this subject as a *Relict Hominoid* without further investigation so I erg the reader to check this one out. I keep going back and

forth.

BIGFOOT MYSTERY MAGAZINE CHRISTMAS ISSUE 2022

YouTube ("North by Wildwest"). 2,586,671 views, posted Oct 3, 2016. 6,067 Comments on the video: Key themes in the comments were that the subject seemed to be very large, glided across rough and snow-ice uneven surface freakishly quickly. Most comments mentioned the dog was scared and the dog owner was concerned over the safety of the dog, some mentioned extended appearing arms and hairy body. Several comments mentioned other undocumented encounters in the Northern Minnesota area. It would take weeks to really analyze the 6,067 comments fully. Perhaps a more in-depth look would be in order when there is more time. I'm still looking for contact information for those involved.

The BFRO data on northern Minnesota: Minnesota has 75 BFRO reports total. Saint Luis County boarders Canada and has 21 BFRO reports.

Montana Christmas Bigfoot Boulder Toss

Here is another possible encounter on Christmas experienced by an old friend of mine when I lived, for s short time, in the Bitterroot Valley in Montana:

"It was on Christmas Eve about 3 years ago, my nephew and his son came over to visit me here in Stevensville, in Raviali County Montana. It had snowed, but not too much to get out and enjoy a bit of snow shoeing around the mountain trails of the Bitterroot Valley. We went into Missoula, where the book and movie a *River Runs through It* took place, and did some last minute shopping and then did some snow shoeing around the Lewis and Clark museum, Bass Creek and a bit along the shore Bitterroot River.

We were snow shoeing on the band for a few hundred yards when were heard a big thud noise, you know how in the snow everything is really quite? Well the snow insolates noise so sound often doesn't carry very far. We paused but there were no more thuds so we kept on our way. We got to a frozen section of the river and we could see an elongated boulder had been tossed out a fair distance onto the ice, we surmised that was the thud we had previously heard. The snow was on top of a brush area in line with the boulder, and its skid pattern, so it must have been thrown quite a ways. It is nearly impossible to pick up a boulder this size even when they are not frozen to the ground, let alone thrown this far. We were a bit weary of looking around on the other side of the snow covered brush patch, as if this was a Bigfoot or a nutty human, it was as strong as an ox. That was the extent of our possible encounter and made for great conversation of Christmas dinner that year."

I have since heard stories boulders being thrown just a short distance from there in Blodgett Canyon and even experienced it myself there in 2014. I checked the BFRO website and we were fascinated to see two more sightings, or encounters in Ravalli County. One of these encounters actually involved seeing a Bigfoot doing a road crossing in the fall of 2005 near Conner, Montana, a truck driver and his wife spring across highway 93 just 40 feet in front of their rig along the

Bitterroot River. The other BFRO sighting in Ravalli County was in

BIGFOOT MYSTERY MAGAZINE					CHRISTMAS ISSUE 2022

he fall of 1991 when a hunting guide recalls encountering a Bigfoot crouching behind a root ball in Bowls Creek. Like the famous Patterson and Gimlin the guide was on horseback and the Bigfoot was behind a root ball. This Bigfoot was human-like with 6 to eight inches of reddish-brown hair all over its' body.

In neighboring Missoula County, a similar rock-throwing encounter, took place in June of 2018, this one by campers on the edge of the Lolo National Forest at the Rattlesnake Wilderness. The Campers heard loud heavy walking and rocks were thrown at their tent, trees were violently snapped off and softball sized rocks were piled into their bucket latrine. The BFRO also documents an actual sighting near the same area, the Rattlesnake Wilderness, this one was way back in 1977 from a young horseback rider. BFRO has seven other encounters in Missoula County all in the summer except none. The BFRO site includes 53 reports inside Montana's geographic bounties, estimates of the breeding population, based on statements of high profile investigators, I would suggest perhaps 300 individuals with a range of a circumference of 65 miles, this would bring some of these individuals into the surrounding states, especially the North Idaho pan-handle, that is highly wooded with 27 inches of rain and 42 inches of snow, well within John Green's famous article 20 inches of rain theory. The high number of fair weather encounters in Montana suggests two possibilities; the first is that Bigfoot hibernates, or at least honkers down in the winter, and two; Bigfoot is migratory and migrates into north Montana in the warmer months and out in the colder months, possibly fallowing resources or a milder climate, I believe many researchers put the geographical range of Bigfoot at approximately 65 square miles.

Bigfoot Christmas

M	E	L	D	R	U	M	U	B	P	N	C
H	S	J	S	N	U	Y	E	B	A	Y	H
B	M	E	A	M	Z	T	E	N	T	T	R
K	E	S	S	A	E	T	H	N	T	S	I
E	A	U	Q	E	R	A	F	A	E	K	S
E	B	S	U	S	E	P	M	M	R	T	T
R	O	B	A	G	P	I	R	W	S	K	M
C	M	I	T	B	I	G	F	O	O	T	A
F	I	R	C	H	Q	M	L	N	N	U	S
F	N	T	H	E	E	E	L	S	S	S	T
U	A	H	F	H	M	Y	S	I	B	A	R
L	B	D	T	A	M	E	B	U	N	R	E
B	L	A	M	I	S	T	L	E	T	O	E
I	E	Y	E	R	E	I	O	H	M	A	H

BIGFOOT
CHRISTMAS TREE
JESUS BIRTHDAY
SASQUATCH
MELDRUM
YETI
ABOMINABLE
SNOWMAN
BLUFF CREEK
PATTERSON
GIMLIN
PATTY
OHMAH
MISTLETOE
PEREZ

BIGFOOT MYSTERY MAGAZINE — CHRISTMAS ISSUE 2022

Sasquatch Christmas

T	I	F	K	D	R	O	L	S	M	U	A
G	Z	A	I	R	T	O	F	K	E	K	G
M	T	N	N	F	F	B	O	O	H	C	N
J	N	T	S	D	O	O	U	O	O	I	I
O	A	Z	B	N	F	G	K	K	M	N	D
H	R	B	E	F	N	G	E	U	A	T	N
N	K	I	T	E	Y	Y	M	M	N	N	A
G	R	G	H	T	K	C	O	N	G	I	T
R	E	F	L	G	N	R	N	A	E	A	S
E	V	O	E	I	O	E	S	M	R	S	D
E	O	O	H	F	E	E	T	E	M	K	D
N	R	T	E	T	L	K	E	E	I	D	O
N	G	S	M	S	T	O	R	R	M	R	T
E	P	A	K	N	U	K	S	F	C	G	G

- SKUNK APE
- YETI
- SKOOKUM
- BOGGY CREEK
- TODD STANDING
- SAINT NICK
- GROVER KRANTZ
- GIFTS
- FOUKE MONSTER
- MANGER
- JOHN GREEN
- NOEL
- LORD
- BETHLEHEM
- BIGFOOT
- FREEMAN
- DNA

Dr. Jeff Meldrum's RELICT HOMINOID FUN and LEARNING ACTIVITY WORKBOOKS

"ARE THERE HUMAN-LIKE CREATURES STILL LIVING IN THE FORESTS OF THE WORLD TODAY?"

SASQUATCH — YETI — ALMASTY — ORANG PENDEK — YOWIE

Featuring the engaging artwork of Slade Delastrode

Share the adventure!

Young and Old will Explore:
- Biology
- Paleontology
- Ecology
- Culture
- Geography
- History

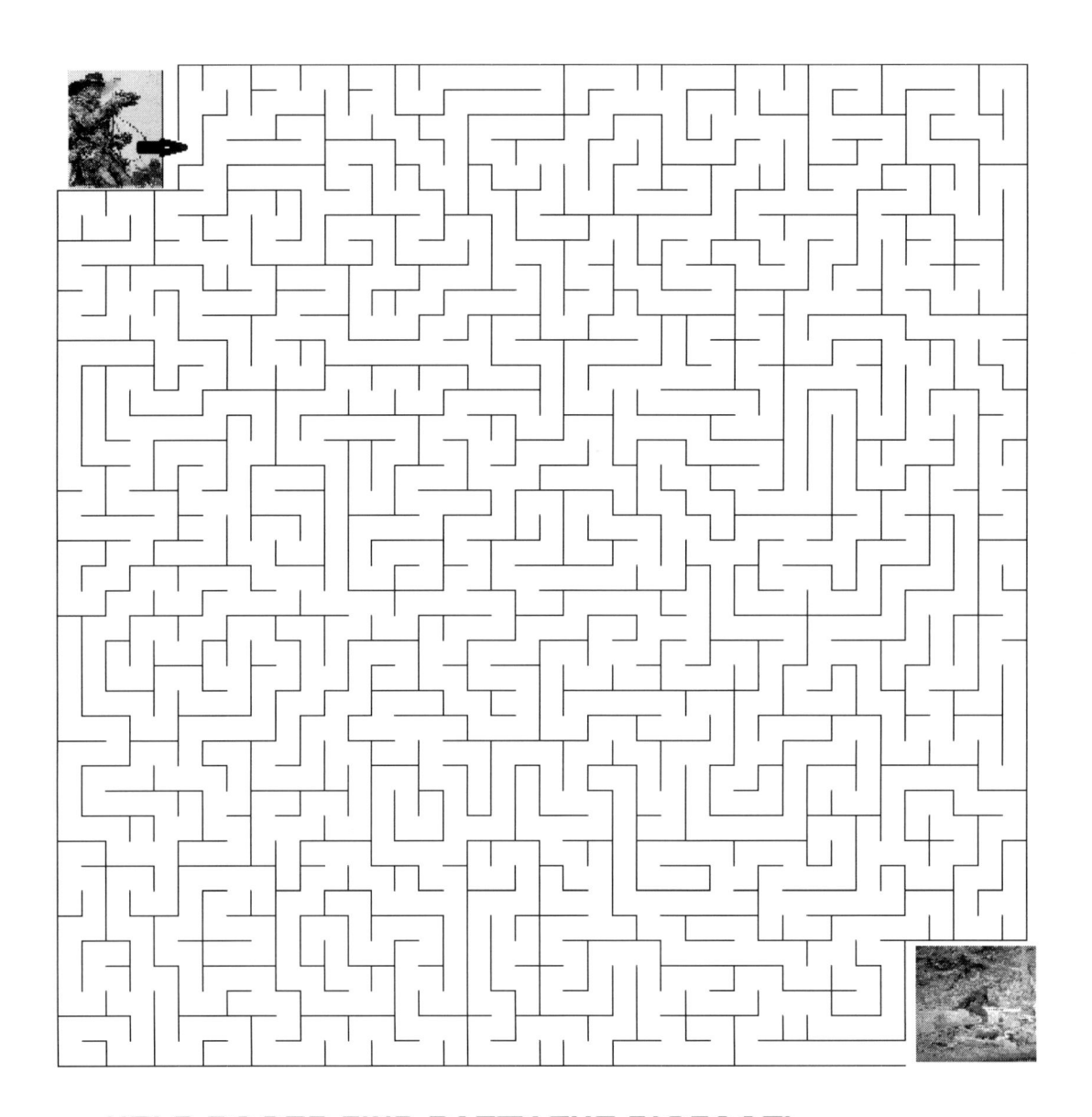

BIGFOOT MYSTERY MAGAZINE					CHRISTMAS ISSUE 2022

HELP ROGER FIND PATTY THE BIGFOOT!

BIGFOOT MYSTERY MAGAZINE   CHRISTMAS ISSUE 2022

HELP BIGFOOT GET HOME FOR CHRISTMAS DINNER!

BIGFOOT MYSTERY MAGAZINE   CHRISTMAS ISSUE 2022

BIGFOOT MYSTERY MAGAZINE   CHRISTMAS ISSUE 2022

On AMAZON BOOKS!

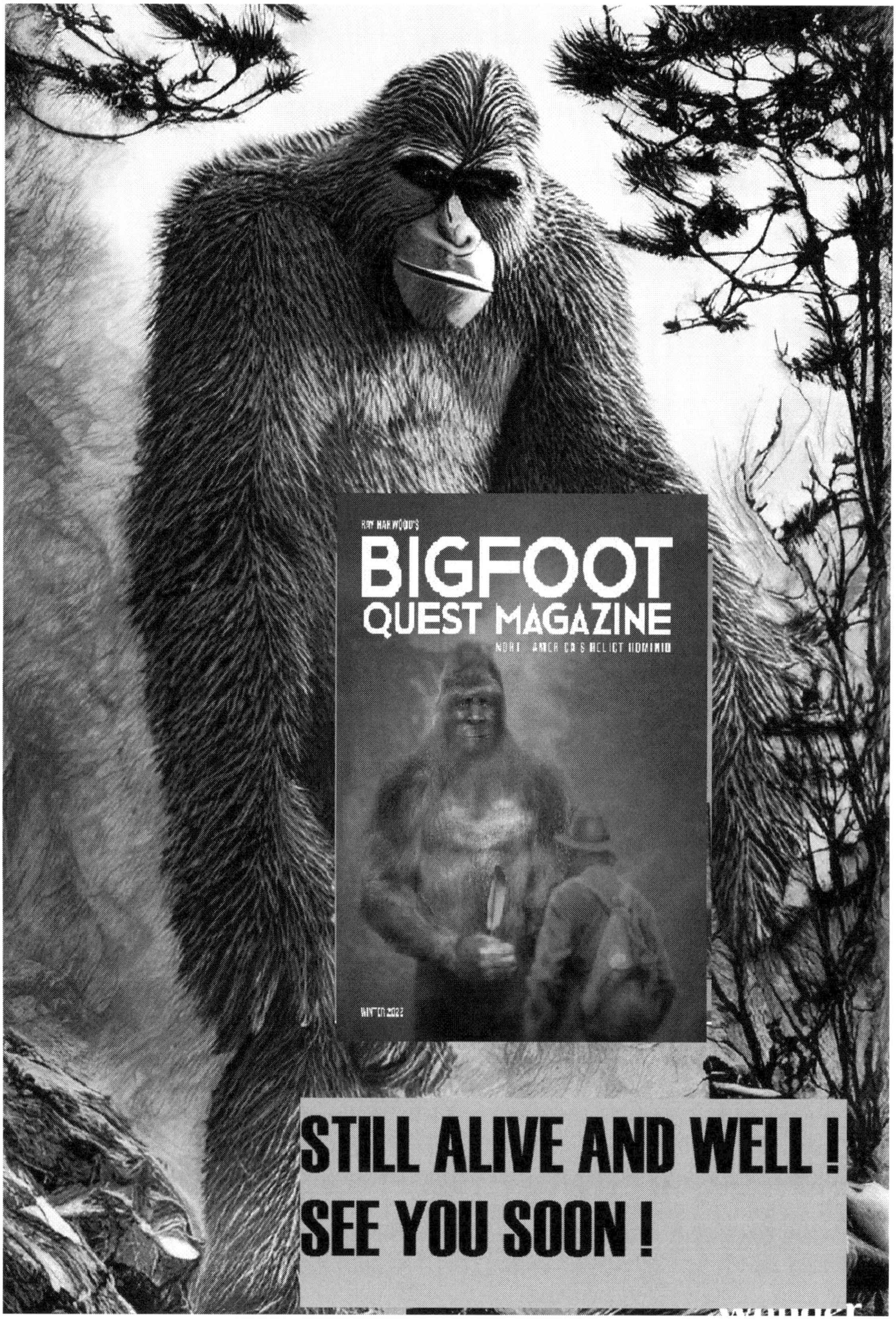
BIGFOOT
QUEST MAGAZINE
STILL ALIVE AND WELL !
SEE YOU SOON !

ALL STILL AVAILABLE ON AMAZON. PERFECT FOR XMAS!

BIGFOOT MYSTERY MAGAZINE　　　　　　　　CHRISTMAS ISSUE 2022

BIGFOOT BOOKS

"A USED AND RARE BOOKSTORE IN WILLOW CREEK, CALIFORNIA, BIGFOOT CAPITOL OF THE WORLD"

- HOME BASE OF THE BLUFF CREEK PROJECT AND RESEARCHER, STEVEN STREUFERT
- SEARCH REQUESTS FOR HARD-TO-FIND TITLES ARE GLADLY ACCEPTED.
- THE STORE IS CURRENTLY OFFERING BIG DISCOUNTS ON BULK PURCHASES.
- DEALERS AND COLLECTORS ARE WELCOME.
- WE SELL ALL KINDS OF BOOKS ON ALL KINDS OF SUBJECTS.
- CURRENTLY THE STORE IS ONLINE AND BY APPOINTMENT.

VISIT:
BIGFOOT BOOKS
40600 Highway 299,
P.O. Box 1167
Willow Creek,
CA 95573-1167,
USA.

CALL: 707-267-4646

CONTACT: bigfootbooks@gmail.com

BLOG: bigfootbooksblog.blogspot.com

BLOG: bluffcreekproject.blogspot.com

34 | Page

Beautiful hand crafted art from a master craftsmen, sorry these are probably back ordered for this Christmas, but contact Bigfoot Taxidermy and get on the list for a future purchase, these are a high demand Christmas present for sure, I am thinking the coolest Bigfoot item a collector could possess. I thank local craftsman - artist Jeff Irvin for his kind authorization to include these photos, please check out his website and if you want one of his masterpieces, or a cool T-shirt get on the list !

Bigfoot Taxidermy, your destination for quality life-sized Cryptid replica shoulder mounts. The story begins in 1775, when Daniel Boone led frontiersmen into Kentucky to clear the way for settlers. On his journey he faced many dangers, not the least of which was the Cherokee and Shawnee tribes. Legend has it that he faced an even greater danger... the mythical Bigfoot. Traveling through what is now the Daniel Boone National Forest; Daniel Boone reportedly shot and killed one of these creatures in the same national forest where these replicas are made. Hopefully, no more Sasquatch will be shot and killed and a Bigfoot trophy should only be a replica hanging on your wall and not a real Bigfoot. These look real but are not, excellent for theme parks, or a great conversation piece that can really get the conversations started! I would get one for my corporate office if I had an office.

BIGFOOT MYSTERY MAGAZINE   CHRISTMAS ISSUE 2022

BIGFOOT MYSTERY MAGAZINE   CHRISTMAS ISSUE 2022

Handcrafted by local craftsman and artist Jeff Irvin in the heart of the Daniel Boone National Forest, the very same where Boone encountered the creature, you won't get any closer to seeing a Bigfoot for yourself. Made with a mix of Italian polymers with a fiberglass cast, assorted foams,paints and sealants with other finishes and synthetic gorilla fur, this is the only safe way to get close to one of these miraculous creatures. How much do these cost?

The Bigfoot cost is $2,599 shipped in the US, with a $1,500 deposit when work begins on your order. Due to the size, weight, and value of the mounts, shipping is expensive, and is included in the price. If you'd like to inquire about international shipping, please contact us.

Werewolf/Dogman mounts are $2,250 lower USA shipped. Contact me to be put on waiting list. International orders contact for price.

How do I order one?   If you're interested in purchasing, please text us at (606) 356-1126 or email jeff@bigfoottaxidermy.com, to receive in stock notifications, or to discuss custom/special orders. What payment methods do you accept?   We currently accept checks via mail or payment through Venmo, we also accept payment through PayPal (PayPal fees will apply).

Is there a waiting list?   Yes, please text us at (606) 356-1126 or email jeff@bigfoottaxidermy.com to get on the list and let us know what you would like.   For special orders/requests, please contact us.What materials do you use?   The replicas are created using a polyurethane cast and coated in fiberglass , assorted foams, paints and sealants with other finishes and synthetic gorilla fur with custom glass eyes. Cpmpletion takes 6 to 8 weeks 8.

BIGFOOT MYSTERY MAGAZINE CHRISTMAS ISSUE 2022

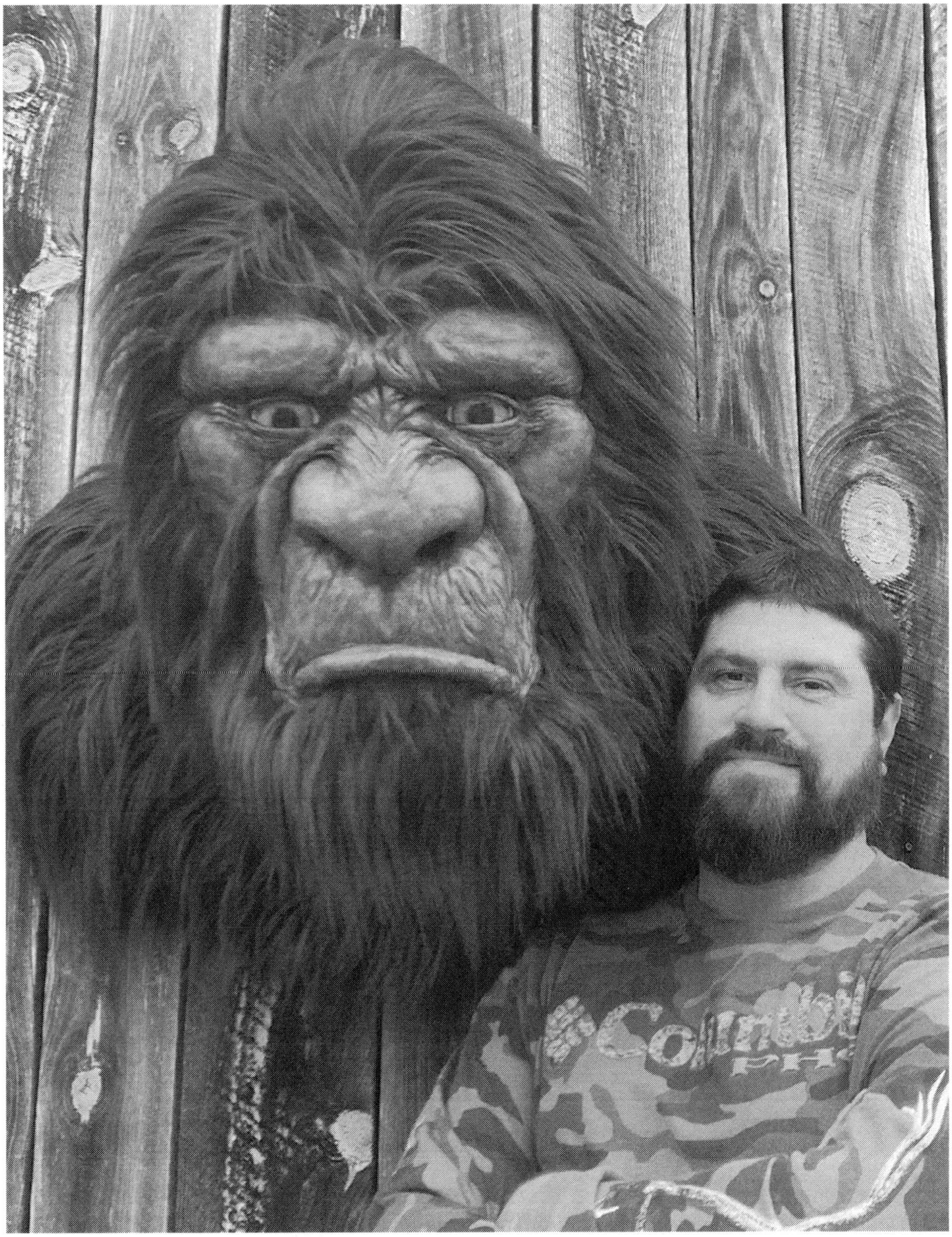

BIGFOOT MYSTERY MAGAZINE   CHRISTMAS ISSUE 2022

Raven Hawk's magnificent artwork is a reflection and expression of the natural beauty of the mountains and forests of northern Idaho wilderness and of the shamanic tradition that inspires, nurtures, and enlightens her. She draws from a profound personal integration with the myriad flora and fauna that surrounded the 100-year-old homestead on which she used to live. Always acutely attuned to the magic and mystery of the Spirit World, Raven Hawk conveys her reverence for nature and her shamanic insights in her brilliant creations. Her love of color allows her to use the full pallet of nature's splendor in the vibrant pieces, she creates, imbuing much of the artist's spiritual persona in every unique piece

Hello Fellow Cryptid lovers, I am currently adding stores to sell my art in.There is not much in them yet but I will be adding new art daily. Please come and visit and share with your friends. Happy Questing the next adventure is right around the corner.
Raven Hawk

I do banners and logos for social media.
Please email me or find me onfacebook.

VISIT MY FACEBOOK TO FIND MY STORES

HTTPS://WWW.FACEBOOK.COM/PROFILE.PHP?ID=100084994565978

rainbowmoonraven@gmail.com

BIGFOOT MYSTERY MAGAZINE   CHRISTMAS ISSUE 2022

RAY HARWOOD'S
BIGFOOT MYSTERY MAGAZINE

SKUNK APES

Wonder

BIGFOOT MYSTERY MAGAZINE   CHRISTMAS ISSUE 2022

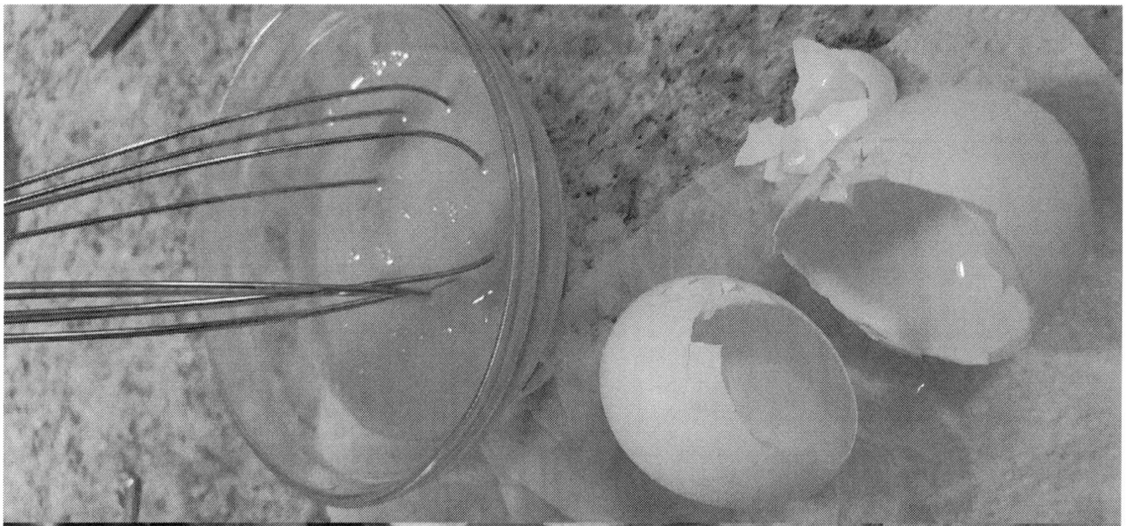

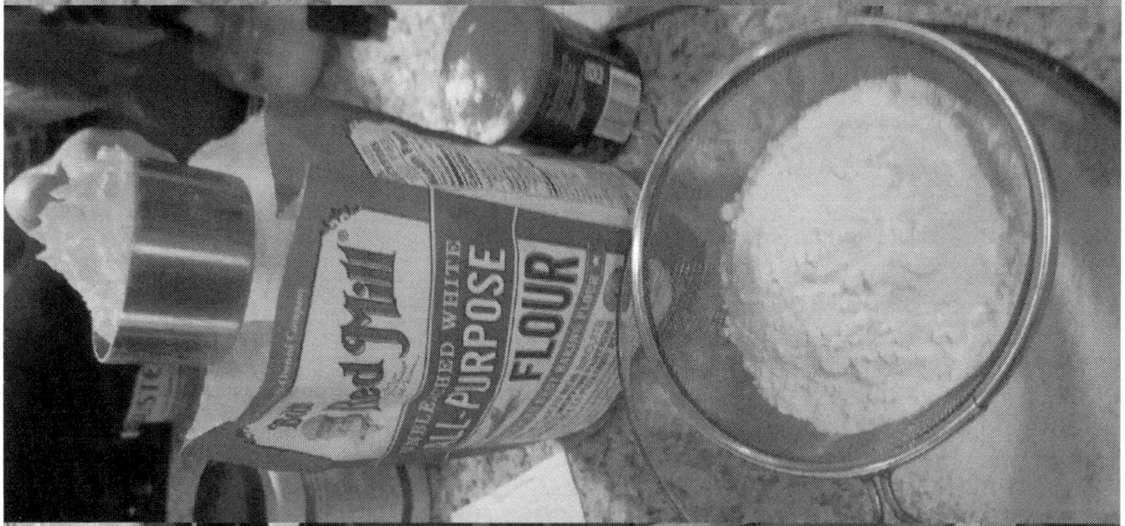
FLOUR

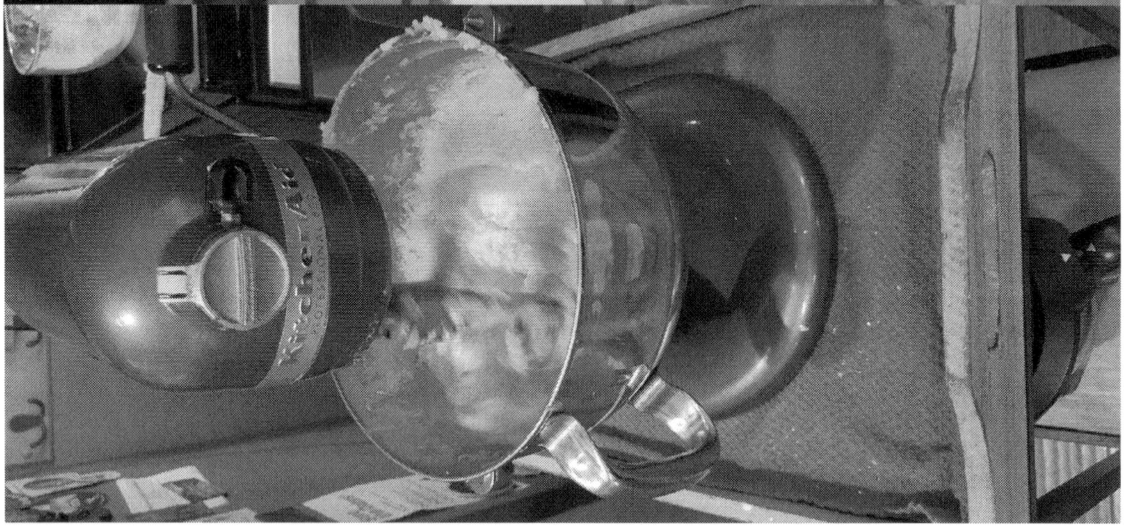

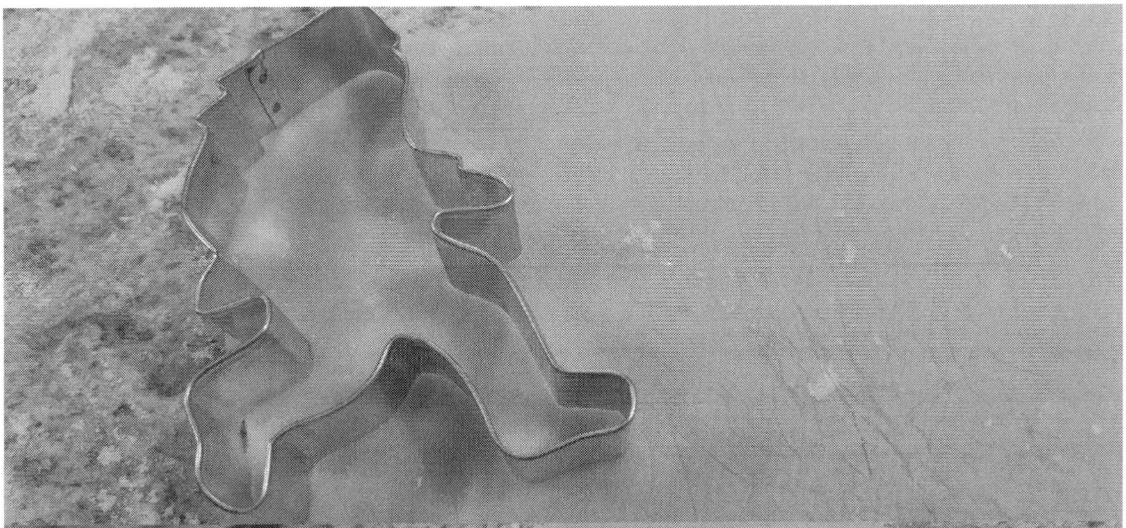

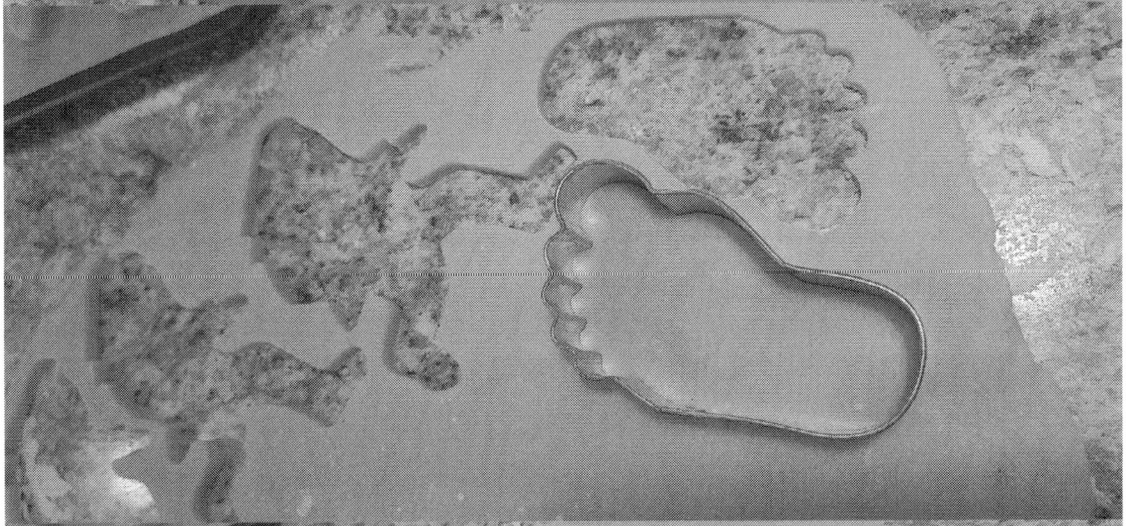

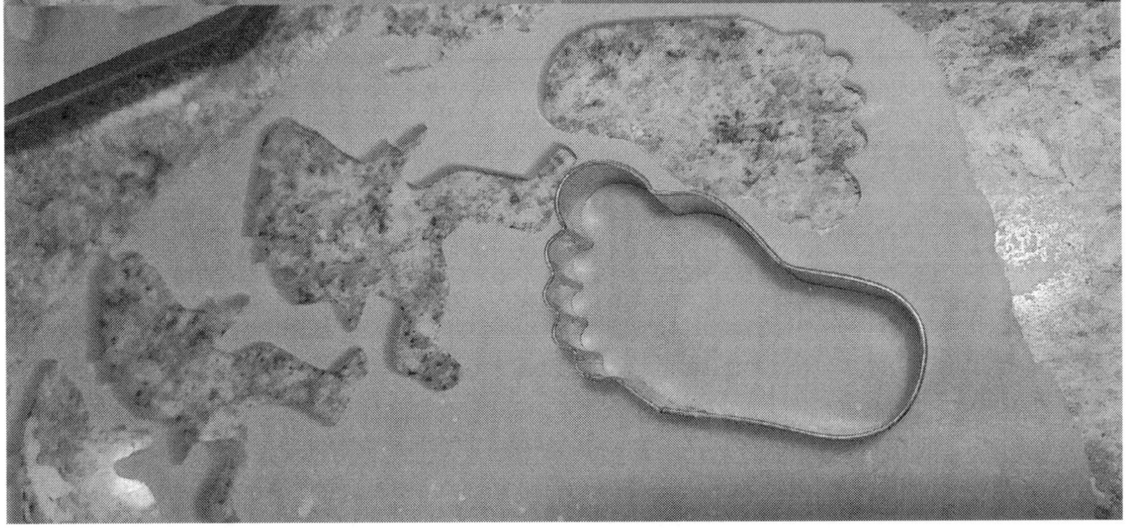

BIGFOOT MYSTERY MAGAZINE   CHRISTMAS ISSUE 2022

48 | Page

BIGFOOT MYSTERY MAGAZINE					CHRISTMAS ISSUE 2022

49 | P a g e

BIGFOOT MYSTERY MAGAZINE　　　　　　　　CHRISTMAS ISSUE 2022

Wonder

50 | P a g e

Bigfoot Sugar Cookies with Ann Cark Cookie Cutter 3-piece set. $11.99 from Amazon.com

Combine butter and sugar in the bowl of a stand mixer (or in a large bowl and use an electric hand mixer) and beat until creamy and well-combined.

Add egg and vanilla extract and beat until completely combined.

In a separate, medium-sized bowl, whisk together flour, baking powder, and salt.

Gradually stir dry ingredients into wet until dough is smooth and completely combined.

Lay out a large piece of plastic wrap and transfer approximately half of the dough onto the wrap.

Cover dough with clear wrap or wax paper and mold . but don't roll it into a flat slab yet. Wrap tightly. Repeat with remaining cookie dough in another piece of wrap. Transfer dough to refrigerator and chill for at least about 3 hours.

Once dough has finished chilling, preheat oven to 350F (175C) and line a baking sheet with parchment paper. Set aside for now.

Dust a clean surface with flour and place one chilled cookie dough round disk onto the surface. Lightly flour the dough and roll out to ⅛" Add additional flour as needed both on top of and beneath the dough so that it doesn't stick.

Use Ann Cark Cookie Cutter 3-piece Bigfoot themed set to cut out squatchy shapes and use a spatula to transfer primate shapes to prepared baking sheet, Bigfoot spacing at least 1" apart.

Bake them Bigfoot critters in the oven on 350F (175C) for 8-10 minutes (this is for cookies that are approximately 3" [7.6cm]; note that smaller cookies will need less time and larger cookies will need more), or until edges just begin to turn lightly golden brown.
Allow cookies to cool completely on cookie sheet before decorating.

We cheated on the frosting and just bought the canned unhealthy kind. Once the frosting got stiff we combed in some lines to dublicate flowing squatch hair

If you want to use the Bigfoot cookies for Christmas orniments add corn starch into the dough, this makes them very hard and tast really bad. I tried to eat one of the corn starch ones and I had heart burn for a week! The eatable ones just made me gain a couple holliday pounds.

Have some of the Bigfoot fans among the kids set some out for Santa Claus!

BIGFOOT MYSTERY MAGAZINE   CHRISTMAS ISSUE 2022

The world famous stopmotion- claymation film *Red-Nosed Reindeer* is a 1964 Christmas animated television special that was produced by Videocraft International, Ltd, currently distributed by NBC Universal Television Distribution . The classic film first aired December 6, 1964, on the NBC television network in the United States and was sponsored by General Electric under *The General Electric Fantasy Hour*. The special was based on the 1949 Johnny Marks song "Rudolph the Red-Nosed Reindeer" which was itself based on the poem of the same name written in 1939 by Marks' brother-in-law, Robert L. May for the Montgomery Wards catalog. Rudolph no longer airs just once annually but several times during the Christmas and holiday season. It has been telecast every year since 1964, making it the longest continuously running Christmas TV special in the USA. Roger Patterson's book *Do Abominable Snowmen of America Realy Exist?* Did not come out until 2 years after Rudolf, so Roger Patterson had seen Bumble in the film, unknown which source from which he coined the name "Abominable Snowmen". If anyone ever prooves that the PG film is not real, I say the costume was modeled after Bumble. The character of Rudolf has always been famously contraverial, these controverses, at times, laughable, Ruldolf being said to represent racism or now an LGBG or some thing, all lies, the writer Robert L. May, like almost all of us, was picked on as a kid so that was the just of that. Oddly enough, I fisrt heard the song by the film's snowman narritaor, Burl Ives, not only in the film but Burl Ives was a friend of my dad's and he would to come over and sing to us with his accustic guitar. I was only five so don't remember it much, my parents had six children and in 1964 there were five as my twin brother had passed away, but we were still a good testing ground for Burl. My sisters were teenagers at the time and remember the mini Burl concerts very

well, he was even Santa Claus for us one Christmas. Of course the reason this Christmas film tradition is in this Bigfoot magazine is because it has a member of the family in it! One of the most endrearing characters in the film is a giant white Abomiable Snowman named Bumble. Bumble is not in the fisrt peom booklet, not is it in the song, but a very previlent character in the film. The name Abominable Snowman was first coined in 1921, "Yeti" or "Metoh-Kangmi" in the Tibetan vinacular. Alexander the Great made a request to see a Yeti in 326 BC in Abominable Snowman was said to inhabit the Himalaya region of Tibet and Nepal. In 1951 mountineer Eric Shipton took photos of the footpints the Himalaya region and they were printed in all the world's newspapers. In 1960, Sir Edmund Hillery, the first recorded human to climb Mount Everest, (20 July 1919 – 11 January 2008) was a New Zealand mountaineer, explorer, and philanthropist. searched for the fabled abominable snowman. Footprints and tracks were lated speculated to be from other animals, perhaps a bounding snow lepord . During the expedition, Sir Edmund Hillary also travelled to some remote temples which contained some alledged "Yeti scalps"; Hillary back three Yeti relics , two were shown to be most probably from bears and one from a possible mountain or domesticated goat or antelope. Hillary said after the expedition: "The yeti is not a

strange, superhuman creature as has been imagined. We have found rational explanations for most yeti phenomena"

Anthony B. Wooldridge In early March, 1986, while undertaking a moutaineering journey to raise money for an organization, Traidcraft, which supports self help projects in developing countries, to obtain first-hand knowledge of the way of life in Himalayan mountain villages operated. Anthony B. Wooldridge observed and photographed a large *Relict hominoid*, a Bigfoot sort of animal which was believed to be the legendary Yeti. According to the wrtittings of Anthony B. Wooldridge .This remarkable encounter occurred by chance during a solo trip in the Garhwal Himalaya of northern India, near western Nepal.

Anthony B. Wooldridge statement of the form of the Yeti is descrobed here from *An encounter in Northern India* by Anthony B. Wooldridge (Source: Cryptozoology, 5, 1986, 63-76.)

" The most compelling evidence for the Yeti explanation is the similarity between other reports of footprints and sightings and the footprints and the general appearance of the animal which I observed. The single footprint of a left foot shows a large impression caused by the big toe, which is well separated from, but parallel with, the other toes. Behind it is a curious depression. These features are very reminiscent of Eric Shipton's photograph taken in 1951 on the Menlung Glacier, although the detail of the other toes is much clearer in the latter photograph than in mine."

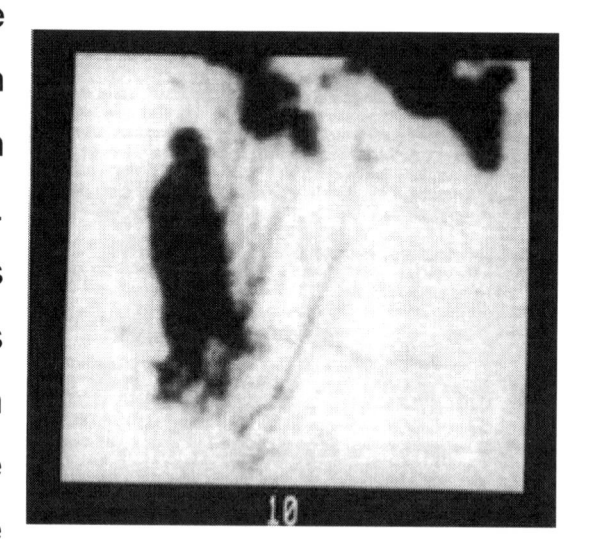

As for the animal's general appearance, it is very much in line with the general consensus of a large animal capable of standing erect in an almost human posture, and with a powerful chest and long arms. What is particularly remarkable is the similarity with the creatures described by Slavomir Rawicz in his 1956 book *The Long Walk*. He mentioned specifically that the heads were squarish, and that, seen in profile, the back of the head was a straight line from the crown to the shoulders. This squareness was one of the features which I noticed immediately. Rawicz claimed to have observed the creatures for 2 hours in 1942, without once seeing them drop onto their hands, and he said that "their interest in the humans seemed to be of the slightest." This was also the impression that I gained, since the creature seemed more interested in looking down the avalanche than at me. Rawicz noted that the animal's shoulders sloped sharply down to a powerful chest. Most of the body was covered with a tight, close fur, but this was mingled with long, loose, straight hairs hanging downwards which had a light grayish tinge as the light caught them. Similar lightish hairs might be the explanation of the lighter band around the crown of the animal I observed, although, with the sun behind the animal, it was difficult to distinguish small color variations. Rawicz's narrative has been criticized for technical inaccuracies in parts, but his description of the creatures is so similar in points of detail to my own experience that it is difficult for me to dismiss. (Photo 1:Unidentified tracks in snow at 3,300 meters observed by Anthony B. Wooldridge. Photo 2: View across the avalanche debris. Arrow indicates figure presumed to be a Yeti observed by Anthony B. Wooldridge. Photo 3: - Digitally processed image of the figure. (Harwell Laboratory, UKAEA). Some researchers have suggested the Yeti in the photo is an anthropometric rock.

Yoshiteru Takahashi is the head of "Yeti Project" in Japan. In 2008 Yoshiteru Takahashi began displaying photographs of what he claims are Yeti footprints. Takahashi claims he first saw a Yeti in 2003. According to Animal Planet he claimed to have first seen Yeti footprints in 1994. Yoshiteru Takahashi took a seven-man team far up the Himalayas where he found the Yeti tracks, 8-inch footprints, which, he claims, could not possibly be those other animals. Takahashi's belief is that the Yeti is around 5 feet tall, much smaller than emence "Bumble" from the Rudolf movie.

A millionaire and Texan oil man, Tom Slick, Jr. was not your typical jr Ewing from the old TV Series; Dallas, Tom Slick, Jr. was not like most of us in vision as a millionaire flying off to Epstein Island or buying off crooked positions. Tom Slick, Jr. was a philanthropist, adventurer, peace advocate and traveler, and for our purposes he was most known for his fascinating contributions in the world of cryptozoology, most often noted for his historic Nepalese missions in search of the Yeti.

Tom Slick Junior's interest in cryptozoology greatest adventures would be in Nepal on the hunt for the Yeti, after his graduation from the academic halls of Yale, in 1956, the "Abominable Snowman" was on Tom Slick Junior's list of things to do! Yeti is like a massive snow Bigfoot (also known locally as Meh-teh, which translates to "man bear."). The Yeti was also documented by Eric Shipton, while attempting to climb the world's highest peak, Mount Everest, Eric Shipton took the first pictures of Yeti tracks. Sir Edmund Hilary, in 1953 climbed to the peak of Mount Everest he came across similar tracks. Sir Edmund Hilary even gazed upon Yeti itself !

In Tom Slick Junior's earlier trips to India he had heard stories about the ape man of the Himalaya Mountains and he wanted some of that action and Bigfoot Goodness! In my article "From Yale to Yeti" I delve more into this in more detail. Tom Slick Junior eventually came to the conclusion that there were two kinds of Yeti. One was about eight feet tall and black while the other was smaller, and reddish in color. The website "Bigfoot 411" the blogger states that there are similarly four types of the American Bigfoot. Tom Slick Junior also photographed and made plaster casts of some of the footprints he had found in the ground in Nepal, Tom Slick Junior also collected droppings and hair allegedly from Yeti. In Nepal, while taking a bus up a steep mountainside, the vehicle lost its brakes and Tom Slick Junior was badly injured. Not being able to search much with his injuries he enlisted the help of the famous Hollywood actor Jimmy Stewart. Tom Slick Junior asked Jimmy Stewart, the actor from the Christmas movie *A Wonderful Life,* to help him steel some evidence from the mummified Yeti hand, at a monastery in Pangboche. Stolen was the thumb bone and phalanx from the "Pangboche hand", Jimmy Stewart replaced the parts with human bones, and then Jimmy Stewart smuggled the Yeti hand parts out of the country hidden inside his luggage.

Because of the injuries in the bus accident and local laws made inhibiting his hunts, Tom Slick Junior was unable to return to Nepal, Slick turned his attention to the American Yeti, the Sasquatch. He could head field expeditions himself in the Pacific Northwest and he indeed endeavored to persevere bring along the "Four Horseman", and he did, discovering many tracks and making many casts and unleashing the Four Horsemen into the world of Bigfoot research. Tom Slick Jr. was killed in 1962, when his Beechcraft airplane crashed in Montana, but this did not end the ride of the Four Horsemen.

"The Four Horsemen" are four were of the pioneers of Bigfoot research: Peter Byrne, John Green, Grover Granz and Rene Dahinden Bigfoot researcher Peter Byrne was born in Ireland. Following service in the Royal Air Force during World War II, Byrne went to Northern India to work on a tea plantation. Peter discovered his first yeti footprint in Nepal in 1948. In 1953 he started his own safari company which he ran for eighteen years. In 1957 Byrne embarked on a three year expedition to hunt and track down the yeti; said expedition was funded by Texas oilman Tom Slick. In 1960 Peter headed another expedition to uncover Bigfoot in the Pacific Northwest of Northern California; other members of the team briefly included fellow Sasquatch researchers John Green and Rene Dahinden.

This expedition was also funded by Tom Slick. In 1968 Byrne co-founded the International Wildlife Conservation Society, Inc. and serves as the executive director to this very day. In the 1990s Peter devised the Bigfoot Research Project, which was a full-scale scientific investigation centered on proving the existence of Sasquatch. The Mt. Hood, Oregon-based operation was ahead of its time in its use of helicopters, state-of-the-art infra-red sensors, and a 1-800-BIGFOOT phone number. Byrne was interviewed in the documentaries *"The Force Beyond"* and the delightfully quirky *"Sasquatch Odyssey: The Hunt for Bigfoot."* He's also the author of the book "*The Search for Bigfoot: Monster, Myth, or Man?*". Now retired, Peter Byrne lives in Los Angeles, California

John Willison Green (February 12, 1927 – May 28, 2016) was a Canadian journalist and a leading researcher of the Bigfoot phenomenon. Green was a graduate of both the University of British Columbia and Columbia University and compiled a database of more than 3,000 sighting and track reports. Green first began investigating Sasquatch encounters and track evidence in the year 1957. He eventually met fellow Canadian Bigfoot enthusiast René Dahinden and the two joined forces and began interviewing multitudes of Bigfoot witnesses. About a year later, John Green was shown a series of 15" Bigfoot tracks crossing a sandbar beside Bluff Creek in California. Green also investigated the tracks reported in Bluff Creek, California in the summer of 1958. In 1963 John Green was elected Mayor of the Village of Harrison Hot Springs where he was owner/operator of the local newspaper, Green did Bigfoot research on the side. Later, after Green researched the Patterson Gimlin encounter in 1972, Green sold his local paper business in order to pursue his passion of Sasquatch research and to write about this at length.

As a world renowned authority on Bigfoot, Green appeared as a keynote speaker at several Sasquatch symposiums. John Green also authored several Sasquatch books on Bigfoot: *The Apes Among Us* (1978), regarded by the Bigfoot Field Researchers Organization (BFRO) as the "best written book on the subject". *On the Track of the Sasquatch (*1968) and *Encounters with Bigfoot* (1980). John Green was one of several researchers featured in the film *Sasquatch Odyssey*, a documentary Bigfoot themed film by a Canadian named Peter von Puttkamer whom was known for his unique style network TV documentaries including the BBC and Discovery Channel.

Rene Dahinden was born August 22, 1930. Mr. Dahinden was born in the town of Weggis, Switzerland, in the district of Lucerne. Rene' moved to Canada in 1953, but made many trips all around the world promoting Bigfoot. For gainful employment Mr. Dahinden worked on a dairy farm in Alberta, Canada.Rene Dahinden became interested in Bigfoot soon after moving to Canada from Switzerland. It began with chance CBS news broadcast on the radio about an expedition to search for Yeti in the Himalayas.

Rene was talking to his dairy farm boss, Wilbur Willich, about how it would be something to go to the Himalayas and "search for that thing".Mr. Willich replied "Hell, you don't have to go that far. They got them things in British Columbia".

Around 1956 Rene Dahinden met British Columbia researcher John Green and the two of them hit it off right away and they began conducting Bigfoot field research together.

Rene' Dahinden conducted decades of field research, witness interviews, taking photos of tracks and making plaster cast, all the while promoting the idea of Sasquatch being a real creature.

In 1967 when the Roger Patterson- Bob Gimlin Bigfoot film came out, many took sides about the film, if it was real or not. Dahinden became a supporter and advocate of the film and wanted to bring the scientific attention to it that he thought it deserved. It is noted that Dahinden and Green showed the Patterson-Gimlin film at several events and to many people around the world, Dahinden even showed it in Russia. Dahinden estimated the weight of "Patty" the Bigfoot, the animal seen in the Patterson-Gimlin film, to be about 700 pounds.

Rene Dahinden acquired copyrights to the photographic images of the Patterson–Gimlin footage and it is believed by some that today Rene Dahinden's estate still apparently owns 51% of the rights to the Patterson-Gimlin film. Frame 352, the famous turn, is in public domain.

In 1973 Rene Dahinden's classic book *"Sasquatch"* with the help of Don Hunter The book covers the classic Bigfoot stories of the Ape Canyon Bigfoot attack at Mount Saint Helens in Washington State in

1924, the strange Albert Ostman Kidnapping also taking place in 1924 in British Columbia, the Baumann attack, Cripple-foot tracks, and the 1967 Patterson-Gimlin film.

Dr. Grover S. Krantz was born in 1931 in Salt Lake City. He obtained an M.A. in anthropology from the University of California at Berkeley and then got his PhD from the University of Minnesota. He was a professor at Washington State University for 30 years and retired in 1998. Grover Kranz stood by the scientific evidence he had gathered to support the existence of Sasquatch. He eventually traveled to Russia and China to investigate large bipedal ape like animals there. When he died his skeleton was put in a glass case with the skeleton of his dog at the Smithsonian Institute, so you can go visit him there if you'd like. (Source: *The Fifth Horseman*, BMM 3; Interview with Daniel Perez).

BIGFOOT MYSTERY MAGAZINE	CHRISTMAS ISSUE 2022

BIGFOOT MUSEUMS:

These are museums that specialize in the curation and study of artifacts that were allegedly made or used by
The American relict hominoid known as Bigfoot or Sasquatch:

Bigfoot Discovery Museum
5497 Highway 9
Felton, CA 95018

Expedition Bigfoot: The Sasquatch Museum
Cherry Log, Georgia:
1934 GA-515
Blue Ridge, GA 30513

North American Bigfoot Center
31297 SE, US-26,
Boring, OR 97009

Crossroads of America Bigfoot Museum
1205 East 42nd St.
Hastings, Nebraska 68901

Cryptozoology & Paranormal Museum
328 Mosby Ave
Littleton, NC 27850

International Cryptozoology Museum,
4 Thompson's Point Road, Suite 106
Portland, ME 04102.

Bigfoot Collection Museum
Willow Creek, CA

Willow Creek China Flat Museum
Willow Creek, CA
http://bigfootcountry.net/

Sasquatch Outpost
Bailey, CO
https://www.sasquatchoutpost.com/

Official Skunk Ape Headquarters
Ochopee, FL
https://www.skunkape.info/

Museum of the Weird
Austin, TX
https://www.museumoftheweird.com/

BIGFOOT PODCASTS :

These are high quality talk shows that focus mainly, or a good portion, on the American relict hominoid known as Bigfoot or Sasquatch:

Bigfoot and Beyond with Cliff & Bobo.
Coast to Coast AM with George Noory.
Sasquatch Syndicate.
The Bigfoot Collectors Club.
Monster X Radio.
SasWhat: A Podcast about Bigfoot.
Sasquatch Chronicles.
Wild Thing.
Bigfoot Eyewitness Radio.
Bigfoot: Terror in the Woods.
Apes Among Us.
Monstrosity with David Race.
Nite Callers Bigfoot Radio.
Monsters Among Us.
Destination Sasquatch.
The Confessionals.
This Paranormal Life.
The No Such Thing Podcast .
Cryptid Campfire.
World Bigfoot Radio.
The Paranormal Podcast with Jim Harold.
Monsterland Podcast.
The Bigfoot Show.

Discovering Bigfoot

CONFRENCES/ SEMINARS/GATHERINGS:

The COVID-19 restrictions are varied in each state.
Variations on local medical mandates, such as social
distancing, vaccine status and or mask requirements,
Are varied in each state.

Confirmation that the event will occur is a must.

Alabama

Bama Bigfoot Conference

Date: No calendar date, nor confirmation that this event will occur this year. No data was available at time of publishing. Please check web sources.

Location Historical Looney's Tavern

Houston, Alabama

The COVID-19 restrictions are varied in each state,
Confirmation that the event will occur is a must.

Arkansas

Ouachita Bigfoot Festival & Conference

Location: Mena, Arkansas

Date: No calendar date, nor confirmation that this event will occur this year. No data was available at time of publishing. Please check web sources.

142 Polk Road 185

Mena, AR 71953

Website: https://blueziplinefarm.com/ouachita-bigfoot-festival-conference

For more info call The Blue; Zipline & Farm at 479-216-8639

The COVID-19 restrictions are varied in each state,

Confirmation that the event will occur is a must.

Fouke Monster Festival

Date: Date: No calendar date, nor confirmation that this event will occur this year. No data was available at time of publishing. Please check web sources.

Location: Fouke, Akansas

The COVID-19 restrictions are varied in each state,

Confirmation that the event will occur is a must.

CALIFORNIA

Bigfoot Daze

Date: Saturday of Labor Day Weekend

Location: Willow Creek, CA

PO Box 704, Willow Creek, CA 95573

(530) 629-2693

info@willowcreekchamber.com

The COVID-19 restrictions are varied in each state,

Confirmation that the event will occur is a must.

COLORADO

Bigfoot Days

Date: April 1-2, 2022– IF NOT CANCELED DUE TO COVID-19

Location: Estes Park, CO

events@estes.org - General Inquiries, Sponsorship, Vendor, & Entertainment

kshea@estes.org - Sales & Booking Information

Phone: 970-586-6104

Fax: 970-586-3661

Estes Park Events Complex

1125 Rooftop Way

Estes Park, CO 80517

The COVID-19 restrictions are varied in each state,

Confirmation that the event will occur is a must.

FLORIDA

The Skunk Ape of Florida Announcing the third annual "Great Florida Bigfoot Conference" April 22, 2023 at the World Equestrian Center in Ocala, FL Featuring an all-star lineup of Bigfoot researchers, investigators, and authors ready to interact with fans and discuss their experiences and findings. Doors open at 9 am and we go until 6 pm. gatherupevents.com/florida-bigfoot-conference/

SWFL Skunk-Ape/Bigfoot Town Hall Conference (unknown for 2023)

GEORGIA

Georgia Bigfoot Conference

No calendar date, nor confirmation that this event will occur this year. No data was available at time of publishing. Please check web sources.

Location: Clayton, G

Rabun County Civic Center

201 W Savannah St.

Clayton, GA 30525

https://georgiabigfootconference.com

The COVID-19 restrictions are varied in each state,

Confirmation that the event will occur is a must.

IDAHO:

Bigfoot Rendezvous 22

Bannock Park County Event Center

10588 Fair Grounds Drive

Pocatello, Idaho

September 23rd and 24th 2022

Tickets/Info:sasquatchprints.com

With Dr. Jeff Meldrum and Cliff Barackmam

Squatch Con Boise

No calendar date, nor confirmation that this event will occur this year. No data was available at time of publishing. Please check web sources.

Location: Fairview, ID

Address: Downtown Nampa

(1st Street S between 12th & 13th Ave)

Nampa, ID 83651

The COVID-19 restrictions are varied in each state,

Confirmation that the event will occur is a must.

Jeff Meldrum, PhD

Professor of Anatomy & Anthropology

Dept. of Biological Sciences

Idaho State University

921 S. 8th Ave., Stop 8007

Pocatello, ID 83209-8007

208-282-4379

-Various personal engagements-

The COVID-19 restrictions are varied in each state,

Confirmation that the event will occur is a must.

KENTUCKY

Wildman Days

No calendar date, nor confirmation that this event will occur this year. No data was available at time of publishing. Please check web sources.

Location: Lawrenceburg, KY

https://www.wildmandays.com

The COVID-19 restrictions are varied in each state,

Confirmation that the event will occur is a must.

MICHAGAN

Marinette/Menominee Bigfoot Convention

No calendar date, nor confirmation that this event will occur this year. No data was available at time of publishing. Please check web sources.

Location: Menominee, MI

(Little Nugget Golf Course)

(906) 864-4653

County Road 338, Menominee, Michigan 49858

The COVID-19 restrictions are varied in each state,

Confirmation that the event will occur is a must.

NEBRASKA

Nebraska Bigfoot Conference

No calendar date, nor confirmation that this event will occur this year. No data was available at time of publishing. Please check web sources.

Location: Hastings, NE

1205 E. 42nd St.

Hastings, NE 68901

https://nebraskabigfootmuseum.com

The COVID-19 restrictions are varied in each state,

Confirmation that the event will occur is a must.

NEWYORK

Sasquatch Festival & Calling Contest

No calendar date, nor confirmation that this event will occur this year. No data was available at time of publishing. Please check web sources.

Location: Whitehall, NY

Skenesborough Park

Whitehall, NY 1288

David Molenaar at 518-499-0874 or

Jason laMoy at 518-223-5460.

www.facebook.com/CallingTheBeast.

The COVID-19 restrictions are varied in each state,

Confirmation that the event will occur is a must.

NORTH CAROLINA

WNC Bigfoot Festival

No calendar date, nor confirmation that this event will occur this year. No data was available at time of publishing. Please check web sources.

Location: Marion, NC

https://marionbigfootfestival.com/home/about/\\

The COVID-19 restrictions are varied in each state,

Confirmation that the event will occur is a must.

OHIO

Ohio Bigfoot Conference

Date: Apr 30, 2022

Location: Lore City, OH

Salt Fork State Park Lodge

& Conference Center Lore City, Ohio.

http://ohiobigfootconference.com

https://www.facebook.com/OhioBigfootConferenceSaltFork/

The COVID-19 restrictions are varied in each state,
Confirmation that the event will occur is a must.

OKLAHOMA

Honobia Bigfoot Festival & Conference

No calendar date, nor confirmation that this event will occur this year. No data was available at time of publishing. Please check web sources.

Location: Honobia, OK

Contact :Christ 40 Acres 580.244.3473

https://www.honobiabigfoot.com

The COVID-19 restrictions are varied in each state,
Confirmation that the event will occur is a must.

OREGON

Oregon Bigfoot Conference

Date: No calendar date, nor confirmation that this event will occur this year. No data was available at time of publishing. Please check web sources.

Location: Canby, OR

The COVID-19 restrictions are varied in each state,
Confirmation that the event will occur is a must.

Blue Mountain Bigfoot Fest

Date: No calendar date, nor confirmation that this event will occur this year. No data was available at time of publishing. Please check web sources.

Location: Baker City, OR

The COVID-19 restrictions are varied in each state,

Confirmation that the event will occur is a must.

Oregon Bigfoot Festival

Date: No calendar date, nor confirmation that this event will occur this year. No data was available at time of publishing. Please check web sources.

Location: Troudale, OR

The COVID-19 restrictions are varied in each state,

Confirmation that the event will occur is a must.

PENNSYLVANIA

Bigfoot BBQ UFO Festival

No calendar date, nor confirmation that this event will occur this year. No data was available at time of publishing. Please check web sources.

(841) 257-0131

Gearhart's Milton Loop Campground

114 Milton Loop Campground Ln.

Location: Dayton, PA

The COVID-19 restrictions are varied in each state,

Confirmation that the event will occur is a must.

SOUTH CAROLINA

South Carolina Bigfoot Festival

No calendar date, nor confirmation that this event will occur this year. No data was available at time of publishing. Please check web sources.

Location: Westminster, SC

The COVID-19 restrictions are varied in each state,

Confirmation that the event will occur is a must.

TENNESSEE

Smoky Mountain Bigfoot Conference

Date: June 23, 2022

Location: Gatlinburg, TN

Gatlinburg Convention Center

234 Historic Nature Trail, Gatlinburg, TN 37738

https://gatherupevents.com/smoky-mountain-bigfoot-conference/

The COVID-19 restrictions are varied in each state,

Confirmation that the event will occur is a must.

TEXAS

Southeast Texas Bigfoot Conference

Date: No calendar date, nor confirmation that this event will occur this year. No data was available at time of publishing. Please check web sources.

Location: Huntsville, TX

3925 SH 30, Huntsville, TX 77340

https://bigfooteruption.com/usa/gulf/texas/southeast-texas-bigfoot-conference/

The COVID-19 restrictions are varied in each state,

Confirmation that the event will occur is a must.

Southeast Texas Bigfoot Presents:

Bigfoot Roadshow / Mineola, Texas

Fri, Apr 29, 2022, 6:00 PM –

Sat, Apr 30, 2022, 6:00 PM CDT

114 North Johnson Street

Mineola, TX 75773

https://www.eventbrite.com/e/southeast-texas-bigfoot-presents-bigfoot-roadshow-mineola-texas-tickets-189924137207

The COVID-19 restrictions are varied in each state,

Confirmation that the event will occur is a must.

VIRGINIA

VA Squatch Fest

Date: No calendar date, nor confirmation that this event will occur this year. No data was available at time of publishing. Please check web so

urces.

Location: Weyers Cave, VA

http://www.vabigfootcon.com/

ecbro98@gmail.com

Weyers Cave Community Center

The COVID-19 restrictions are varied in each state,

Confirmation that the event will occur is a must.

Virginia Bigfoot Con:Date: June 18th 2022:Location: Weyers Cave, VA.: http://www.vabigfootcon.com/ecbro98@gmail.com

Our 4th Annual Virginia Bigfoot Conference being held at the Holiday inn & Conference Center in Staunton Virginia.

WASHINGTON:

Yakima Valley Bigfoot Con: Legends Casino: October WWW.LEGENDSCASINO.COM.

Spokane Valley Sasquatch Roundup:June 17th 2023. Meldrum. (907) 505-0951

Squatch Fest January 28th 2023:Cowlitz County Even Center. Longview Event Center:(360) 423-8400

NW Sasquatch2.Clup: Marblemount Sasquatch Conference August (360) 873-2238

Neah Bay Sasquatch & Nature's Bounty September www.neahbaywa.com

Metaline Falls Bigfoot Festival. June 17, 18 2023: mfbigfoot.com

BIGFOOT MYSTERY MAGAZINE　　　　　　　　　　CHRISTMAS ISSUE 2022

(Too　　　　　　　much　　　　　　　eggnog!)

BIGFOOT MYSTERY MAGAZINE CHRISTMAS ISSUE 2022

BIGFOOT MYSTERY MAGAZINE   CHRISTMAS ISSUE 2022

BIGFOOT MYSTERY MAGAZINE

HAPPY NEW YEAR!

HAVE A GREAT 2023

Wonder

BIGFOOT MYSTERY MAGAZINE CHRISTMAS ISSUE 2022

Wonder

BIGFOOT MYSTERY MAGAZINE   CHRISTMAS ISSUE 2022

Wonder

87 | Page

BIGFOOT MYSTERY MAGAZINE　　　　　　　　CHRISTMAS ISSUE 2022

Wonder

BIGFOOT MYSTERY MAGAZINE   CHRISTMAS ISSUE 2022

Wonder

Wonder

Printed in Great Britain
by Amazon